SACRAMENTO PUBLIC LIBRARY
D0977343

The Weird Sisters
A Note, a Goat, and a Casserole

Owlkids Books acknowledges the financial support of the Canada Council for the Arts, the Ontario Arts Council, the Government of Canada through the Canada Book Fund (CBF) and the Government of Ontario through the Ontario Creates Book Initiative for our publishing activities.

Published in Canada by Owlkids Books Inc., 1 Eglinton Avenue East, Toronto, ON M4P 3A1
Published in the US by Owlkids Books Inc., 1700 Fourth Street, Berkeley, CA 94710

Library of Congress Control Number: 2021942137

LIBRARY AND ARCHIVES CANADA CATALOGUING IN PUBLICATION

Title: The weird sisters : a note, a goat, and a casserole / written by Mark David Smith ; illustrated by Kari Rust.
Names: Smith, Mark David, 1972- author. | Rust, Kari, illustrator.
Identifiers: Canadiana (print) 20210256958 | Canadiana (ebook) 20210256966 | ISBN 9781771474566 (hardcover) | ISBN 9781771475532 (EPUB) | ISBN 9781771475549 (Kindle)
Classification: LCC PS8637.M56524 W45 2022 | DDC jC813/.6—dc23

Edited by Katherine Dearlove | Designed by Elisa Gutiérrez

Manufactured in Guangdong Province, Dongguan City, China, in October 2021, by Toppan Leefung Packaging & Printing (Dongguan) Co., Ltd. Job #BAYDC102

A B C D E F

Conseil des Arts du Canada

Mark David Smith

Illustrations by Kari Rust

OWLKIDS BOOKS

For Barbara, my mother, who would

have liked this —M.D.S.

For Jeff —K.R.

Contents

WELCOME
TO
COVENLY

CHAPTER 1

The Sisters Move In

One spring evening, the town of Covenly gained three new residents: one bony, one round, one whose knuckles rubbed the ground. They looked *weird*. So did their gray cat.

Hildegurp wore sunglasses. Yuckmina's eyeglasses were thick as a thumb. Glubbifer's bangs hung to her nose. And the cat, Graymalkin, had a crooked tail. They all wore tall hats—except for Graymalkin. (Cats, as a rule, are never in hats, despite what you may read.)

The newcomers' strangeness made Rupert Flinch nervous. Rupert was showing them the home at 1313 Jitters Drive. If they bought the house, Rupert would get a fee. With that money,

he could buy more brushes and paint, for when Rupert sold a property, nothing made him happier than to give his buyers the gift of a freshly painted house. But would they buy this house? The yard was overgrown. The windows were broken. The walls leaned.

"Oh dear, oh dear, oh dear!" Rupert said. "I should show you something else!"

"It's perfect!" Hildegurp replied. "We'll live upstairs and run a pet store below."

"An *emporium* of pets!" Yuckmina said.

"Gack!" Glubbifer agreed. Glubbifer did not use words, but she always meant what she said.

"No one has lived here for many years," Rupert explained. "Do you plan to fix it up?"

"Not to worry, Rupert Flinch," Hildegurp said.

"Worry not, Rupert Flinch," Yuckmina said.

"Tsk, tsk," Glubbifer said, wagging her long

finger. She pressed against the porch post, and the roof sagged.

"See?" Hildegurp said. "That's better already! A few more cobwebs, a little less paint, and you'll hardly recognize this place!"

Rupert cleared his throat. "Did you say *less* paint?"

CHAPTER 2

A Strange Greeting

Jessica Nibley had unusual tastes. Her favorite foods, clothes, and books were often out of the ordinary. Not everyone understood her choices. When her parents offered to get her a pet, they imagined a cat, a dog, a fish. Jessica chose a baby goat.

"But *everyone* gets dogs and cats and fish," her parents pleaded.

"Exactly," Jessica replied.

So her parents bought her a baby goat. But now Jessica's baby goat was missing. Who could help Jessica find him? Up the street, the Three

Sisters' Pet Emporium was holding its grand opening. Perhaps the owners could help?

"Our first customer!" Hildegurp cried as Jessica opened the door. Jessica introduced herself.

Yuckmina was stirring a pot on the stove. "Would you like some Hurlyburly Soup? It is nearly ready."

"I'm looking for a kid," Jessica said.

"You *are* a kid," Hildegurp corrected. "And we do *not* sell children."

"Or put them in soup," added Yuckmina.

Graymalkin licked a paw. Glubbifer licked her lips.

"No, no," Jessica explained. "A kid is a baby goat. I had a pet kid, but he's lost."

"A pet goat?" Hildegurp said. "How strange. You need a more sensible pet. How about . . . "

She lifted a possum by the tail. Yuckmina pointed to a scorpion in a jar. Glubbifer raised a box labeled *Fire Ants—Keep Closed!*

Jessica shook her head.

"Perhaps we could make you a frog," Hildegurp suggested.

"You can't *make* a frog," Jessica said.

"No—make *you* a frog," Yuckmina corrected.

Glubbifer pulled a wand from her cloak.

"It's not nice to turn people into frogs," Jessica said. "Don't you know that?"

The weird sisters shrugged.

"We're sorry, Jessica Nibley," Hildegurp said. "We're still learning how not to be bad witches."

"That's good," Jessica said. "I can help you learn."

"We'd like that," Hildegurp said. "And we can help find your kid."

"I'd like that too."

Jessica and Hildegurp shook hands.

"Let's go to my house so you can see where I kept him," Jessica said. She opened the door, but then stopped. She'd spotted a note lying on the porch next to a ceramic dish.

The note was soiled, and many pieces had been torn away. Jessica held it for the sisters to read.

CHAPTER 3

Looking for Trouble

Cosmo Keene lived at 1423 Jitters Drive. He had once been the manager of the toy store. As manager, his favorite things to say had been "Don't touch!" and "No funny business!" People who touched items in the store or created funny business were troublemakers. Cosmo had retired from working, but he still liked to keep watch and protect his community from trouble, just like a sheriff. He also liked black licorice.

He had just sat down to enjoy a nice, chewy rope of licorice when he heard a commotion.

Through his window, he spied Jessica Nibley talking with the weird sisters. The sisters' arms waved about. The big one kept smacking a fist into her open hand.

"Funny business," he said to himself.

He removed a plastic badge from his desk. The word "sheriff" was printed across it in capital letters. He had bought it at the toy store. He clipped the badge to his shirt pocket.

Then Cosmo strode out his front door and marched purposefully up the street, chewing a piece of licorice as he went.

"What's all this ruckus about?" he shouted as he approached the group. "Newcomers, eh? Now, look—this is a quiet street in a quiet town. It is not a place for . . . troublemakers!" He leaned in close, giving the sisters a hard look.

"Oh? Tell me," Hildegurp said, squinting back at him, "how do you like lily pads?"

Hildegurp closed her eyes and murmured. Yuckmina drew a thin wand from a hidden pocket. Glubbifer clenched her fists. Graymalkin coughed up a hair ball and gave it a sniff.

Jessica shook her head at the sisters. "This is our neighbor Mr. Cosmo Keene. Hi, Mr. Keene. Nice to see you."

Hildegurp relaxed her lips. Yuckmina returned her wand. Glubbifer folded her arms. Graymalkin bit at something itchy in her fur.

"Mr. Keene, *we're* not making trouble," Jessica said.

"Oh yeah? Then why aren't you in school? Kids should be in school."

"Kids do not go to school, Cosmo Keene," Hildegurp explained, trying to be helpful. "Kids are baby goats."

"And I'm not in school because it's Saturday," Jessica added.

Cosmo had to think about that one. "Well, as

long as there's no trouble. Still, I'll be watching you!"

"But there *is* trouble," Jessica Nibley said, holding up the note.

It was too late. Cosmo had left.

CHAPTER 4

Of Notes and Pens

"Could Cosmo Keene have written that nasty note?" Hildegurp asked.

"He wasn't very friendly," Jessica agreed. "It's a mystery."

"Two mysteries," Yuckmina said, rubbing her chin. "A mysterious note and a missing goat."

Hildegurp brightened. "What if the one who wrote the note stole the goat?"

Glubbifer smiled. Rhymes always tickled her.

Yuckmina drew a long broom out of her hat and sat on it. It floated. Hildegurp and Glubbifer climbed aboard too. It still floated. "Show us where you keep your kid, Jessica Nibley. We can travel together."

Glubbifer patted an empty spot on the broom. Jessica sat. Graymalkin leaped onto Glubbifer's back. Hildegurp said, "Alakazam!" and the broom zoomed them across streets, past trees, and over houses, sparks streaking behind them. They

whirled to a stop at Jessica's house.

"That was interesting," she said, laughing nervously and picking leaves out of her hair.

"You need a proper hat," Yuckmina said.

"And sunglasses," Hildegurp added.

"Come on," Jessica said. "I'll show you my goat's pen."

"Goat's pen? Your kid can write?" Hildegurp said. "Smart kid!"

"No, a pen is like a cage for larger animals," Jessica explained. "My kid sleeps inside at night where it's safe and warm."

Jessica led the sisters inside the house and introduced them to her mother, who was working at a desk near a window.

"It's so nice that you've found someone to play with," said Mrs. Nibley, looking up from her papers.

Jessica lifted her chin. "We're not playing—we're investigating." Graymalkin hopped onto the windowsill.

"Of course you are, dear," Mrs. Nibley said. "Have fun!" She gathered her papers and left the room.

The sisters inspected the pen carefully. They didn't notice Graymalkin at the window, ears flattened. She stared intently at someone in the bushes outside.

CHAPTER 5

Seeking Answers

Cosmo hid behind a streetlight and peeked out. When it was safe, he darted beside a car, tiptoed behind a garbage can, and leaped into a shrub to spy on Jessica's house.

Chelsea Oh was a teacher who lived nearby. She couldn't see well without her glasses. "Now where did I put them?" Chelsea asked herself. She got down on the floor to feel for them.

She crawled across the kitchen.

She crawled out the door.

She combed the grass and sifted the dirt.

She found something, but it didn't feel like glasses.

"Shoe!" Chelsea said.

"Shoo? Me?" Cosmo replied. "Shoo yourself! Why are you in my shrubbery?"

"Your shrubbery? Oh my! I'm trying to find my glasses," Chelsea Oh said.

"They're on your head," Cosmo observed.

"So they are." Chelsea flicked them onto her nose, then looked around. "Wait—why are you in *my* shrubbery?"

Cosmo pointed at Jessica's house. "I'm spying on troublemakers," he whispered.

Chelsea frowned. "Troublemakers? Here? But our neighbors have always been so kind and welcoming."

"Which is exactly why we should report troublemakers to Officer Nazeri."

"You go ahead," Chelsea said. "I need to figure out where I put my—"

"Glasses?" Cosmo suggested.

"Dish!" she answered. "I couldn't find my casserole dish without my glasses, but now I'll be able to see it. Thank you." She got up and returned to her kitchen, shutting the door behind her.

Only Cosmo saw the strange glow coming from Jessica's windows.

CHAPTER 6

The Sisters Take a Look

"Sisters," Hildegurp said, "we need our Eye."

"Eye?" Jessica asked.

"It is private, Jessica Nibley," Hildegurp said.

"A private eye?" Jessica clarified.

"Yes, very secret. I keep it under my hat."

Hildegurp reached in and removed the Eye. Yuckmina cackled. Glubbifer rubbed her giant hands together.

The Eye glowed a soft pink. The sisters took turns holding it up to the goat's pen like a magnifying glass. They began to chant.

"Show us how to find the goat! Show the author of the note!"

"Show!" Hildegurp cried.

"Show!" Yuckmina shrieked.

"Ow!" Glubbifer yelled. Graymalkin had attacked her foot. The cat liked to pounce on wiggly things.

The sisters moved about the room. They looked at the chair. They examined the desk. They investigated the sofa.

"What do you see?" Jessica asked.

Hildegurp said, "I see . . . furniture." Then the Eye grew brighter. "Wait! Our Eye sees something!"

Pink light streamed from the Eye. It blazed out the windows and across the lawn, then zeroed in on the table in Jessica's living room. More specifically, it focused on a piece of paper on the desk.

"What's happening?" Jessica asked.

"Our Eye sees more than things," Hildegurp said excitedly. "It sees connections. It gives us clues. What is this?"

Jessica lifted the sheet of paper. "This is homework from my teacher. I'm supposed to add up the costs of buying a house. I have to figure out all the fees and the cost of repairs like painting."

"It's a clue!" Hildegurp said. "Rupert Flinch paints houses!"

"He does, sister!" Yuckmina said.

"And does he not also *sell* houses?" Hildegurp asked.

"Right again, sister!" Yuckmina said.

"And did he not try to convince us to buy a *different* house?"

"Mm-hmm," Glubbifer grunted, nodding.

"Could Mr. Flinch have written that mean note?" Jessica wondered.

"We will ask Rupert Flinch about this," Hildegurp said.

CHAPTER 7

The Tell-Tale Clue

Rupert washed his brushes and tossed his dirty water. Unfortunately, he hadn't heard the sisters stomping toward him. Glubbifer was very wet. So was Graymalkin.

"Oh dear, oh dear, oh dear," Rupert said. "Can I get you a towel?"

Glubbifer nodded.

"Never mind that now, Mr. Rupert Flinch," Hildegurp said.

Glubbifer frowned.

"Rupert Flinch, did you leave a nasty note on our porch?" Yuckmina demanded.

"Note? Nope. I did return, but only to paint your house," he said. "I always like to paint a house after I sell it."

"You painted the sisters' house?" Jessica said. "You didn't do a very good job."

Rupert sighed. "Everyone's a critic," he said. "I paint what I see. Perhaps you need to see my work in better light." He disappeared inside, then returned holding an oil painting of the sisters' house.

"Oh!" Jessica said. "You painted a *picture* of their house!"

"How does it look?"

"Peeled and faded, just the way we like it," Hildegurp said.

"Wait—what's this?" Jessica asked, leaning closer to the painting.

The sisters held their Eye up to the canvas. There seemed to be something fluffy just visible on the roof in the picture.

"That doesn't look like part of the house," Jessica said. "I can't tell, but is that a goat's tail?"

"That's not right," Rupert said.

"It certainly is not, Rupert Flinch," Hildegurp agreed. "Baby goats do not tell tales, and they do not write with pens—for they are kids!"

"No," Jessica said. "I mean an animal's tail, not a story tale. If that's my kid on the roof, we've got to rescue him!"

"I'll come too," Rupert said, looking at his painting. "I need to repaint your house."

When he looked up, however, Jessica and the sisters were gone.

CHAPTER 8

Chelsea Has an Idea

Chelsea Oh liked to cook. She also liked children. Now, you can't cook children, but you can teach children to cook. Unfortunately, there were no jobs at her school teaching children to cook. Instead, she taught reading and math. She was Jessica's teacher.

Today she was cooking her favorite: cabbage roll casserole! But wait—hadn't she already made that? She couldn't remember.

"Oh well," she said to herself. "You can never have too much casserole."

The casserole was her mother's recipe, and

her grandmother's before that. But Chelsea was forgetful. She often misplaced her ingredients. At the moment, she had the feeling she'd forgotten something important.

She double-checked her recipe. The sauce had simmered. The rice was ready. The cabbage was cooked. What else was there? All she needed to do was transfer everything to her casserole dish and put it in the oven.

But where was her dish?

It was not in the cupboard.

It was not in the sink.

It was not in her sock drawer.

Where could she have left it? She tapped her forehead, trying to remember.

Just then, something zoomed past her open window with a sound like a rushing wind: ZOOSH! She jumped.

Her curtains flapped.

The grass shivered.

Leaves swirled by.

Whatever it was had zoomed too fast for her to see, but she looked in the direction of the tumbling leaves toward . . . the sisters' old house on the hill.

"Wait just a minute," Chelsea said to herself.

CHAPTER 9

An Opportunity at Last

Officer Golsa Nazeri sat in her police car. The car was parked by the side of the road. Her radar gun was pointed down the street. Her keys were in the ignition. She was ready to catch a speeder.

It would be her first. She had never caught a speeder in Covenly because it was a small town. Most people did not drive. They walked.

"It's my job to keep this town safe," Officer Nazeri thought to herself. "If people would only drive more, I could catch speeders and protect the town."

She looked down the road. She looked up the road. There were no other cars in sight. She sighed.

Someone tapped on her car window. It was Cosmo Keene. On his shirt, he wore a plastic badge that said "sheriff." Officer Nazeri frowned. Cosmo was not a real sheriff. But he was a citizen, and citizens needed to be protected.

Officer Nazeri looked down and pressed the button for her power window.

Something crashed.

Someone screamed.

Officer Nazeri looked up.

Cosmo was gone.

What had happened to Cosmo? She didn't have time to find out. A wild blur was zooming away from her.

"Aha!" Officer Nazeri said. "A speeder!"

She turned the key, and the police car roared to life. She switched on her siren, flicked on her flashing lights, and raced down the road in hot pursuit.

CHAPTER 10

The End of the Chase

While they were flying, the sisters and Jessica had accidentally plowed into something bulky and smelling faintly of black licorice. They had tumbled onto the soft grass near the road, but the broom had kept flying. So they ran instead. By the time they arrived at the sisters' pet emporium they were sweating and panting. (Running is much more tiring than flying on a magical broom.)

"Look!" said Jessica, pointing.

The sisters looked. Sure enough, Jessica's goat was on the roof.

"YEEEEE-OWWW!" someone screamed, streaking past them.

Cosmo zoomed along the street . . . on the sisters' broom!

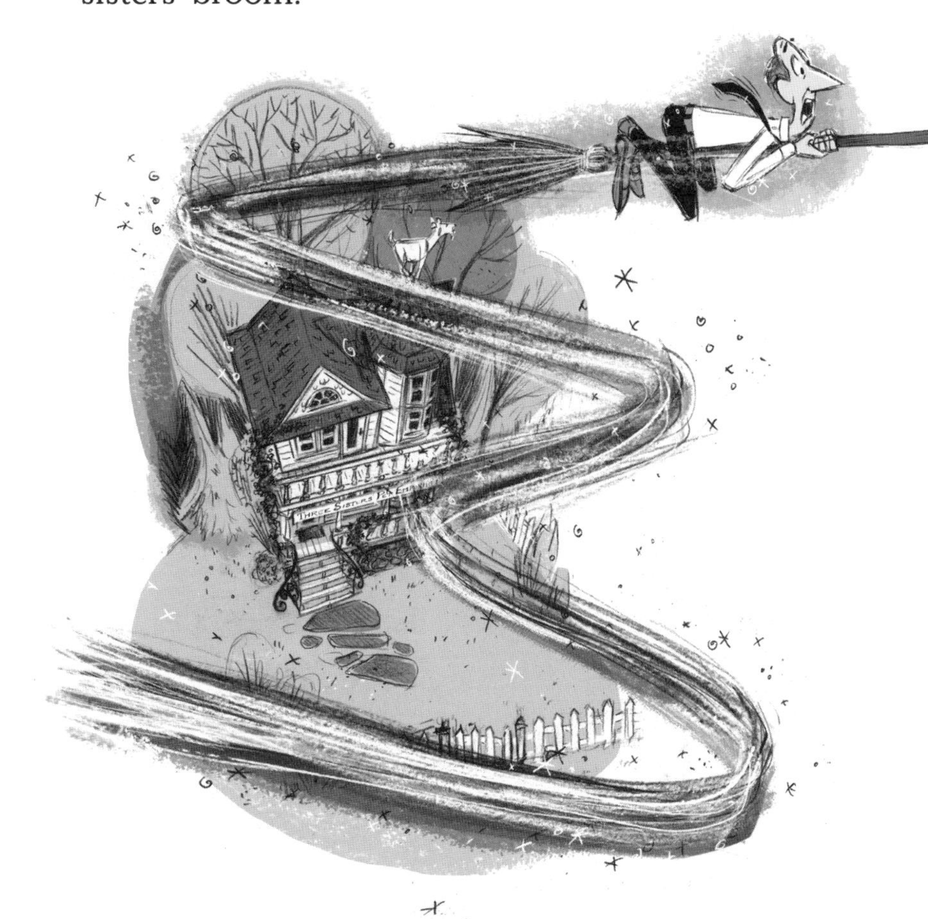

He zigged in front of Jessica's house.

He zagged behind Chelsea's house.

Everywhere he went, Officer Nazeri zigged and zagged below him in her police car. Her siren blared. Her red and blue lights flashed.

"Mr. Keene needs help!" Jessica said.

"Do not fear, Jessica Nibley," Hildegurp said.

"Jessica Nibley, fear not," Yuckmina said.

"Phthbbt," Glubbifer spat, wagging her finger.

The sisters took out their wands and concentrated. Hildegurp muttered. Yuckmina chanted. Glubbifer hummed. Graymalkin sneezed.

They veered Cosmo around. They raced him toward the roof of their house.

"YEEEEE-OWWW!" he yelled again.

He collided with Jessica's goat. The goat clung to him in fear.

"Maa!" cried the goat.

"Aah!" cried Cosmo.

The sisters lowered their wands. The broom carrying the goat and Cosmo descended to a few feet above ground, hovered in midair, then suddenly dropped.

Cosmo landed with a thud.

The goat landed on his chest.

"Kids like high places," Jessica explained.

Cosmo huffed. "No kidding."

CHAPTER 11

Pointed Fingers

Rupert arrived at the sisters' house with his paints, his brushes, his canvas, and his easel. He compared his painting to the sisters' house. There was no animal tail on their roof anymore, but there were a lot of people on the lawn. And one goat. And one cat.

"Oh dear, oh dear, oh dear," he said to himself. "I must repaint this house." He unfolded his easel and chose a fine brush.

Just then, Officer Nazeri's police car screeched to a stop. "Has anyone seen a speeder go by?" she asked.

"Officer Nazeri," Cosmo said, "those sisters used some hocus-pocus to make a broom fly!"

"Hocus-pocus?" Hildegurp said. "How silly! 'Hocus-pocus' is for turning people into frogs. Brooms use 'alakazam.'"

"Officer Nazeri, arrest those weird sisters!" Cosmo shouted. "They are troublemakers!"

"Not anymore," said Jessica. "The sisters are kind and helpful. People can change."

“Yes, people *can* change,” echoed Yuckmina, pulling out her wand and pointing it at Cosmo.

Hildegurp mumbled something quietly. Glubbifer opened a frog-sized jar. Cosmo looked green.

Jessica gave Yuckmina a warning shake of her head. “Not *that* kind of change.”

Yuckmina put the wand away. Glubbifer closed her jar.

“I don’t see any troublemakers, but I did see a speeder,” Officer Nazeri said, eyeing Cosmo. “The law is clear, however: no one may speed with a *motor vehicle*. Brooms don’t have motors, so I cannot issue a speeding ticket.”

Chelsea appeared, marching across the lawn. “There’s my dish!” she said, pointing to the porch. “Did you like my casserole?”

“What casserole?” Hildegurp asked.

“Maa,” said the goat. A curious orange sauce coated the fur around his mouth.

CHAPTER 12

Putting the Pieces Together

Hildegurp reached into her hat and pulled out the Eye. The sisters held it up to the goat and looked.

"This is too big to be a kid," said Hildegurp.

"I guess I didn't notice how much he'd grown," Jessica admitted. "He must have gotten big enough to jump from his pen and climb out the open window."

"And then he ate the casserole," Hildegurp deduced, eyeing the empty dish.

"Hungry kid," Yuckmina said.

Glubbifer whistled for everyone's attention. She held up a small scrap of paper and pointed at the goat. Other scraps of paper stuck to his fur.

"Someone ripped my letter," Chelsea said.

"Chelsea Oh, you wrote that note?" Yuckmina said.

"Of course!" said Chelsea.

Jessica plucked the small torn papers from her goat's fur. She taped them together with the original note.

"Well, we're not leaving, Chelsea Oh," Hildegurp said.

"Wonderful!" said Chelsea.

"Look!" Jessica held up the repaired note:

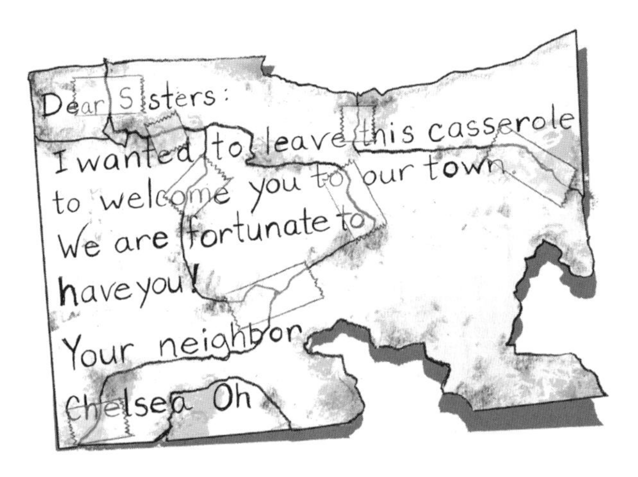

Dear Sisters:
I wanted to leave this casserole
to welcome you to our town.
We are fortunate to
have you!
Your neighbor,
Chelsea Oh

"Oh!" said Hildegurp.

"Ah!" said Yuckmina.

"Ooo!" said Glubbifer.

"I'm sorry you didn't get to try the casserole," Chelsea said.

"It would've been nice to have dinner together, Miss Oh," Jessica agreed.

"We still can!" Hildegurp said. She ran inside and brought a spoonful of soup to her lips. She smiled, then called through the open window, "The Hurlyburly's done!"

"I can stay. My paint needs to dry anyway," Rupert said.

"And I'm finished looking for speeders today," Officer Nazeri said. "May I also have some soup?"

"This isn't finished yet!" Cosmo objected.

"Of course not," Jessica said, looking at the soup. "We haven't even started. You can join us too, Mr. Keene."

They all went inside to share the Hurlyburly Soup—even Graymalkin and Jessica's goat got a bowl.

"This is very nice soup," Cosmo said after a

taste. “Wait—I was mad about something!”

“I’m sure it was nothing,” Hildegurp said, a grin spreading across her face. “Have some more soup.”

Hurlyburly Soup

Original ingredients	Substitutions for hard-to-find ingredients
2 large squirts gall of goat	1¾ cups (425 mL) chicken or vegetable broth
2 large squirts thick gruel	1⅓ cups (325 mL) tomato-vegetable cocktail
1 cup (250 mL) sweltered toad venom	1 cup (250 mL) water
1 root hemlock (preferably dug at night), diced	1 large potato, diced
2 fillets fenny snake, sliced	2 stalks celery, diced
2 slips yew (preferably silvered in the moon's eclipse), diced	2 carrots, sliced
1½ cups (375 mL) dragon's scales	1 (14½ ounce [425 mL]) can diced tomatoes
1 cup (250 mL) wolf's teeth	1 cup (250 mL) chopped green beans
1 cup (250 mL) eye of newt	1 cup (250 mL) corn kernels
wool of bat, to taste	salt and pepper, to taste

What to do

1. In a large cauldron, combine gall, gruel, venom, hemlock, snake fillets, yew, dragon's scales, wolf's teeth, and eye of newt.

2. Season with wool of bat. Boil and bubble, then simmer for 30 minutes, or until the charm's wound up.

If you don't have the original ingredients

1. With an adult's help, combine the broth, tomato-vegetable cocktail, water, and potato in a large pot, and bring to a boil. Simmer for 10 minutes.

2. Add the celery and simmer for 7 minutes, then add the carrots and simmer for another 5 minutes.

3. Add the tomatoes, green beans, and corn kernels, simmering for 4 more minutes.

4. Season with salt and pepper, to taste.

Mark David Smith has never had sisters, but he does have a wife and three children—none of whom are weird. Mostly. And though he has never practiced witchcraft, being an English teacher means he often teaches students to "spell." Mark is also the author of the picture book *The Deepest Dig*. He lives in Port Coquitlam, British Columbia.

Kari Rust loves the "magic" that happens when an illustration comes to life. She conjures art in an old house in Vancouver, British Columbia, where she lives with her husband and two kids. They don't have a pet goat, but they do have a dog who is quite weird. Kari is the author and illustrator of *Tricky* and *The House at the End of the Road.*

Coming Soon

Book two in the Weird Sisters series!

Jessica and the Weird Sisters—Hildegurp, Yuckmina, and Glubbifer—have a new mystery to solve when they discover the town's beloved tire swing lying on the ground, its rope severed. Who would commit such a crime? And why? The foursome fly into action to solve the case as only they can: with outlandish disguises, a mob of unusual pets, a magic potion, and an enchanted lawn mower on the loose. Will they find the swing vandal? Find out in this second charming and hilarious Weird Sisters mystery.

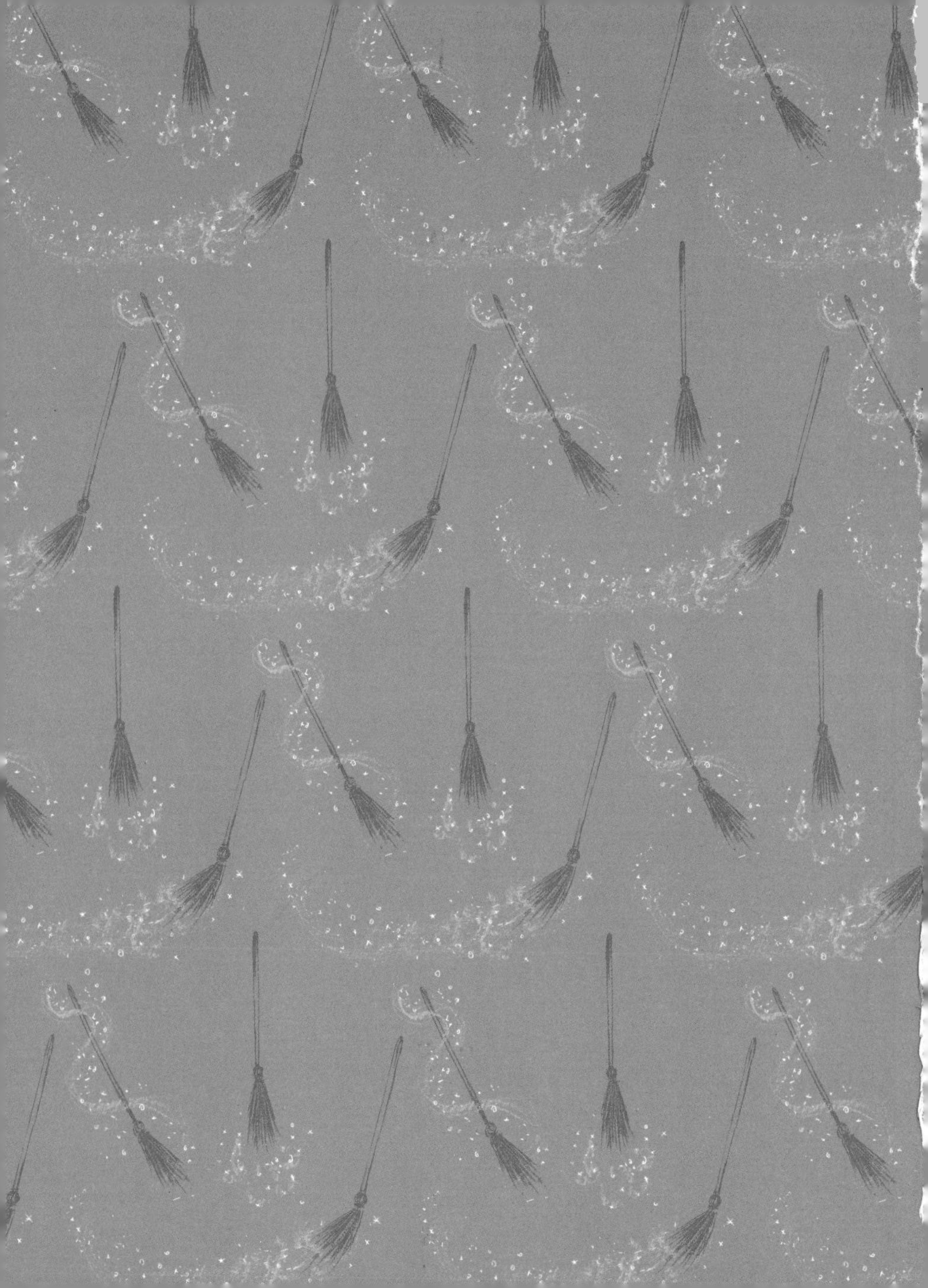